This book belongs to:

_____

Text copyright © 1997 by Callaway & Kirk Company LLC.
Illustrations copyright © 1997, 1994 by Callaway & Kirk Company LLC.

All rights reserved. Published by Scholastic Inc. in association with Callaway & Kirk Company LLC.
Miss Spider and all related characters are trademarks and/or registered trademarks of Callaway & Kirk Company LLC.
SCHOLASTIC, CARTWHEEL BOOKS, and associated logos are trademarks and/or registered trademarks of Scholastic Inc.

150- 4673

ISBN: 0-439-83305-1

11 10 9 8 7 6 5 4 3 2 1   6 7 8 9 10/0

Printed in Mexico
This edition first printing, May 2006

The paintings in this book are oil on paper.

Miss Spider's Tea Party

paintings and verse by David Kirk

Cartwheel
·B·O·O·K·S· ®

Callaway Arts & Entertainment

One lonely spider wished to play.

Two beetles gasped and ran away.

Three fireflies saw her web and fled.

"We won't come in," the four bees said

Five rubber bugs stared silently.

$\mathcal{S}$ix ants refused to drink her tea.

Seven butterflies hid from sight.

Eight tea cakes sat without one bite.

Nine spotted moths appeared but then

In fear, they flew away again.

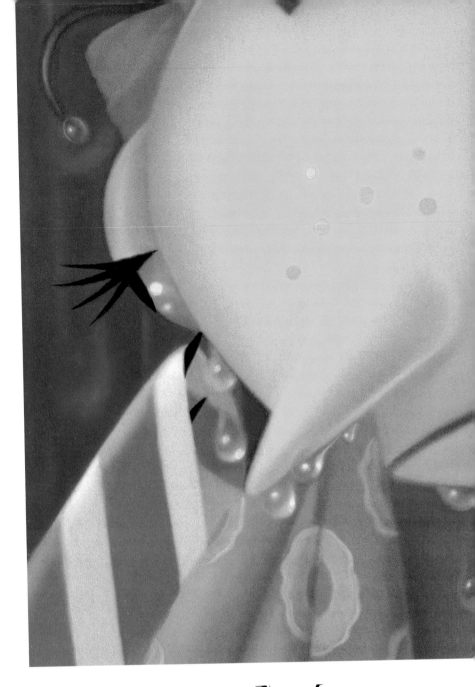

Miss Spider sobb

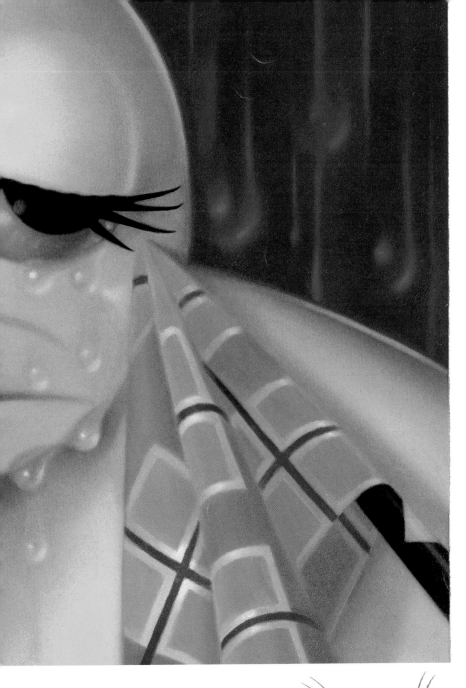

ey've all dashed off."

Across ten cups, she spied a moth.

She dried his wings, then tossed him high.

Next day eleven bugs came by.

Twelve flowers were their gift to say,
"We've heard you're kind. Come on, let's pl